DUDLEY
TOP DOG

In honour of Clifford Davies ~ Top Dog

JD

Scholastic Children's Books
Commonwealth House, 1-19 New Oxford Street
London WC1A 1NU, UK
a division of Scholastic Ltd
London ~ New York ~ Toronto ~ Sydney ~ Auckland
Mexico City ~ New Delhi ~ Hong Kong

First published in hardback in the UK by Scholastic Ltd, 2003
First published in paperback in the UK by Scholastic Ltd, 2003
This paperback edition first published in the UK by Scholastic Ltd, 2004

Copyright © Jo Davies, 2003

ISBN 0 439 98279 0

All rights reserved

Printed in Singapore

2 4 6 8 10 9 7 5 3 1

The right of Jo Davies to be identified as the author and illustrator
of this work has been asserted by her in accordance with the
Copyright, Designs and Patents Act, 1988.

DUDLEY
TOP DOG

written and illustrated by Jo Davies

Hippo

Dudley the dog and
his family sat around the tv,
watching the annual dog show.

"Oh, isn't he handsome!"
said Dudley's dad, as an Alsatian with
sticky-out ears marched into the
arena to collect a bronze medal.
"I'd feel very proud to own
a dog like that."

Dudley felt his own ears,
which flapped around his face.

"I'm not a handsome dog,"
he thought.

"Oh, what a pretty creature!"
said Dudley's mum, as a poodle with
a pom-pom tail trotted into the
arena to collect a silver medal.
"I'd feel very proud to own
a dog like that."

Dudley looked at his own tail,
which was big and bushy.

"I'm not a pretty dog,"
he thought.

"Wow! Look how tall he is!"
said Big Peter, as a Great Dane strolled
into the arena to collect a gold medal.
"I'd feel very proud to own
a dog like that."

Dudley stretched out his own legs,
which were rather stumpy.

"I'm not a tall dog,"
he thought.

"Oh, isn't he smart!" said Little Jo,
as a dotty Dalmatian bounced into the
arena to collect a big shiny trophy.
"I'd feel VERY proud to own
a dog like that."

Dudley peered at his own fur,
which was scruffy and had
no pattern at all.

"I'm not a smart dog,"
he thought.

That night,
when everyone went to bed,
Dudley decided he was going to
make himself into a dog his family
would be proud of.

First he found a can of hairspray.
Spurt! Spurt! Comb! Comb! Spurt! Spurt!

Soon the sticky spray began to harden and
his floppy ears were transformed.
They now stood completely upright
on his head.

"Now I am handsome," he said,
as he admired himself in the mirror.

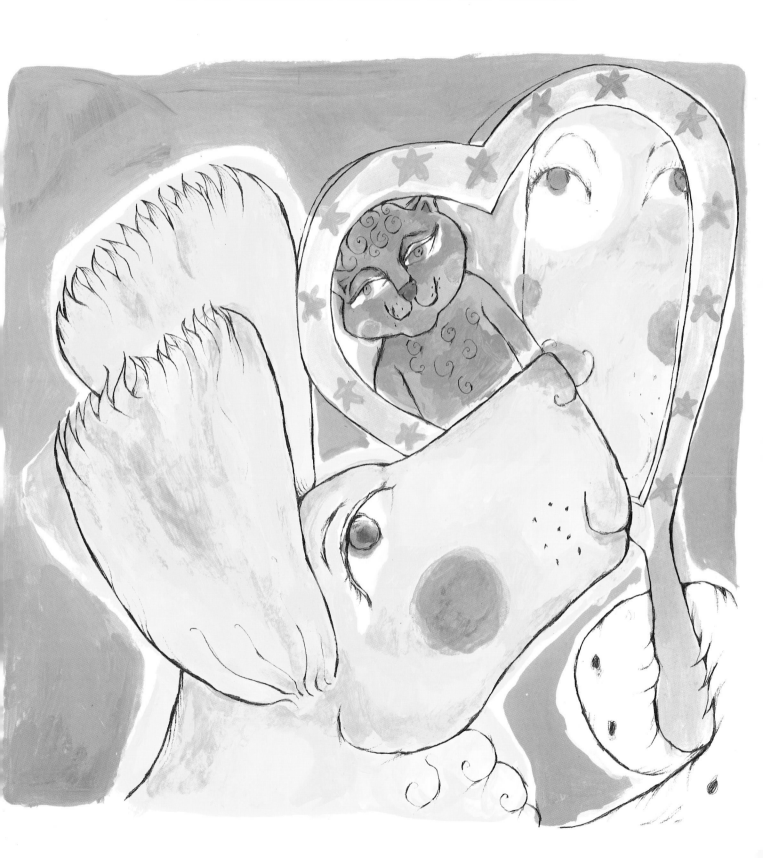

Next
he rummaged
through a big
basket of knitting
and picked six balls
of wool in the
prettiest colours.

Very carefully
he tied a ball
on each of his legs,
one on the top
of his head, and
the last one at the
end of his tail.

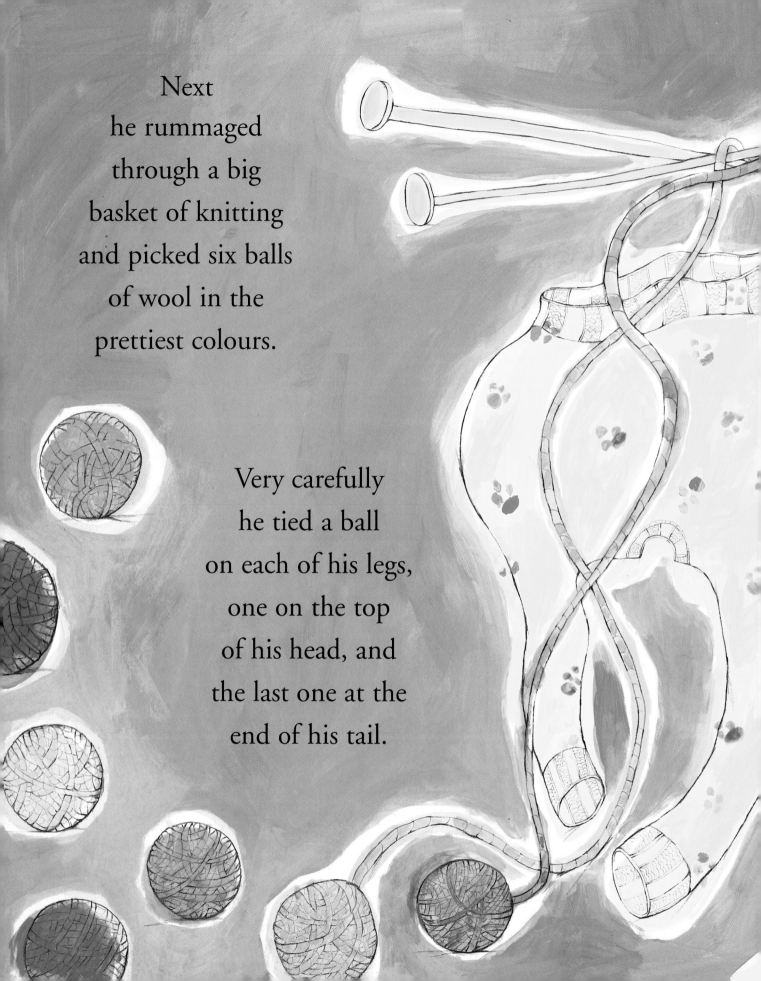

"Now I am handsome and PRETTY," he said,
as he admired himself in the mirror.

Then he opened the door to
the shoe cupboard.

He knew exactly what he was looking
for: two pairs of high-heeled shoes.
Gingerly he put a shoe on each paw.

"Now I am handsome, pretty and TALL,"
he said, as he admired himself in the mirror.

Lastly he went to Little Jo's toybox.
He didn't want building blocks or jigsaw
puzzles. No, this was what he wanted –
a box of paints and a big paint brush.

Eagerly he began to paint
lovely big spots on his coat.

He stood back to have a look.
"Now I am handsome, pretty, tall and
SMART," he said, as he admired
himself in the mirror.

All this work to turn himself into
a dog his family would be proud of was
exhausting, and Dudley felt very tired.
"I need my beauty sleep," he thought,
as he curled up to dream of winning
next year's dog show.

Next morning, when Dudley
heard his family coming down the stairs,
he got himself ready to greet them.

As the door opened he walked forwards,
holding his head high.

But suddenly his ears began
to droop, the balls of wool began
to unravel, and his legs got all tangled.
He wobbled and he teetered on his
high heels, tripped up and knocked
into the goldfish bowl, sloshing water
down his lovely new coat.

At first Dudley's family went very quiet.

Then they began to grin and giggle,
and laugh and squeal, and soon
they were howling with laughter.

It was five whole minutes before they
rushed towards him.

"Oh, Dudley! What an amazing dog!"
said his dad, as the family untangled him
and gave him big hugs.

"You deserve the biggest trophy there is."

"You are the BEST dog in the world.
We are VERY proud to own
a dog like you."